This edition published
by Parragon Books Ltd in 2016
and distributed by

Parragon Inc.
440 Park Avenue South,13th Floor
New York, NY 10016
www.parragon.com

Written by Margaret Wise Brown
Illustrated by Gabriel Alborozo
Edited by Laura Baker
Designed by Ailsa Cullen
Production by Rob Simenton

ISBN 978-1-4748-5743-7

Printed in China

ALL THE FAMILIES

PaRragon

Bath • New York • Cologne • Melbourne • Delhi
Hong Kong • Shenzhen • Singapore

Everyone has a family.

Bunnies
have families.

See the
bunny family with
the nine baby
bunnies.

Dogs have families.

See the dog family with the five baby puppies.

Elephants have families.
See the elephant family with
one baby elephant.

And so have you a family.
Who is the baby?

When it is lunchtime,
and families get hungry,

really hungry,

what do they eat?

The bunny family with
the nine baby bunnies
nibble lettuce.

The dog family with
the five baby puppies
chew five bones.

The elephant family
with the one baby elephant
eat treetop buds.

All the families eat their food,
so YOU eat your food.

When it is nighttime
in the houses,
and in the rooms,
and out of the windows,

when it is really night,
what do the families do then?

The families go to sleep.

The bunny family with the nine baby bunnies
twitch their noses and fall asleep.

The dog family with the five baby puppies
curl up in balls and fall asleep.

The elephant family with the one baby elephant
hang down their ears and go to sleep.

All the families
go to sleep, and YOU
go to sleep.